AF279160

BE THE BEST AT
KARATE
JOHN ALLAN

CONTENTS

www.hungrytomato.com

First published by Hungry Tomato Ltd in 2022
F1, Old Bakery Studios, Blewetts Wharf, Malpas Road, Truro,
Cornwall, TR1 1QH, UK

ISBN 978 1 914087 17 2

A CIP catalogue record for this book is available from the
British Library.

Manufactured in the USA.

Picture credits:
(t=top; b=bottom; m=middle; l=left; r=right; bg=background)
Shutterstock: mejorana (all top tips bubbles); Nomad_Soul
1bg; Vladimir Vasiltvich (front cover)

Every effort has been made to trace the copyright holders,
and we apologize in advance for any unintentional
omissions. We would be pleased to insert the appropriate
acknowledgments in any subsequent edition of this
publication.

Disclaimer: The author, publisher, and bookseller cannot take
responsibility for your safety. When you attempt any of the
exercises in this book, you do so at your own risk.

INTRODUCTION 3

WARMING UP & STRETCHING 4

KARATE TECHNIQUES

Stances 6

Punching 8

Kicking 10

Blocking 16

SKILLS & DRILLS

Footwork Drills 22

Sparring Drills 24

DIET & MENTAL ATTITUDE 30

GLOSSARY & INDEX 32

INTRODUCTION

Karate is an exciting sport, and a traditional martial art with a fascinating history. Karate can be used for self-defense but has many other benefits, such as improving health, physical fitness and boosting self-confidence. The word 'karate' is derived from two Japanese characters: kara, which means empty, and te, which means hand.

ELEMENTS OF KARATE

Karate training is broken down into three sections.

BASICS (KIHON)

These are the fundamental techniques which make up karate, including stances, punches, blocks and kicks. The kihon are presented in the 'karate techniques' section of this book.

FORMS (KATA)

Kata are traditional choreographed sequences of moves performed as if fighting a series of imaginary opponents. The kata contain the self-defense techniques of karate, although understanding them takes years of training.

SPARRING (KUMITE)

The kumite section of karate involves sparring with a partner. At the beginner level, this is simply a set routine of punches and blocks. Some of these are covered in the 'Skills and Drills' section of this book. At the highest level, kumite is an unstructured fighting contest.

ORIGINS OF KARATE

Karate originated in Okinawa, a small island found near China, which is part of modern Japan. The traditional elements of karate were developed in Okinawa but have a strong Chinese influence. Modern elements of karate, such as sports karate and the belt system, originated in Japan.

WARMING UP & STRETCHING

Most karate classes will start with a warm-up and stretching session, and will also often end with more stretches. Stretching is particularly important as it helps to improve your technique and performance in kicks. This is because it improves your flexibility.

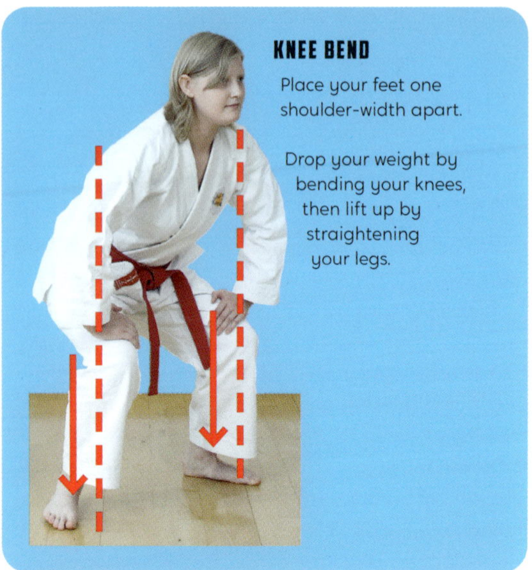

KNEE BEND

Place your feet one shoulder-width apart.

Drop your weight by bending your knees, then lift up by straightening your legs.

STOMACH CRUNCH

Lie on your back with your knees bent and feet flat on the floor. Place your hands on your thighs and lift your upper body, so that your hands reach over your knees. Keep your lower body still.

UPPER BODY ROTATION

Stand with your feet one shoulder-width apart. Put your arms up in front of you with your elbows bent.

Rotate slowly side to side. Let your feet twist as you turn, coming up on the ball of your rear foot.

KNEE LIFT

Stand with your feet shoulder-width apart. Lift your knee, and try to raise it to the same height as your shoulder.

ARM STRETCH

Reach across your body with your arm. Use your other arm to stretch it further by pushing above the elbow.

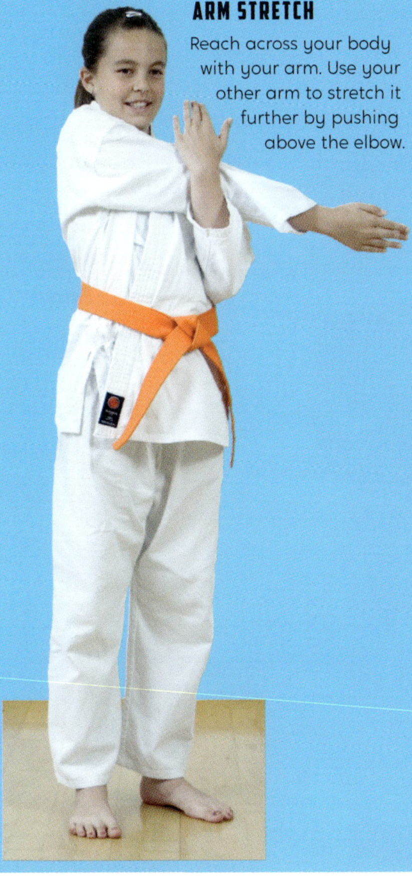

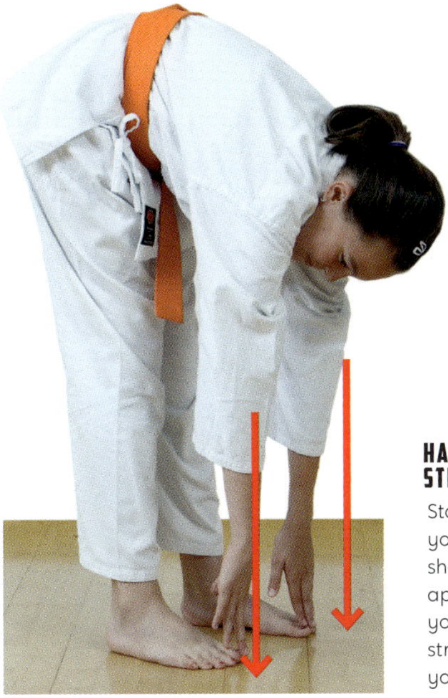

HAMSTRING STRETCH

Stand with your feet one shoulder-width apart. Keeping your legs straight, touch your toes.

QUAD STRETCH

Stand on one leg and lift your other leg behind you. Keep your back straight, and make sure your foot and knee are lifting straight back, not out to the side.

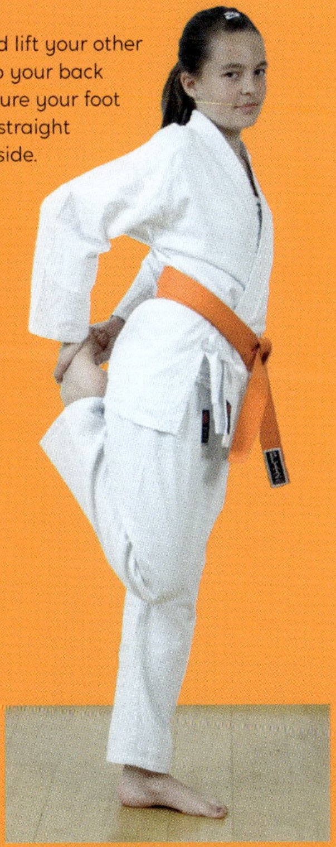

INSIDE LEG STRETCH

Place your feet two shoulder-widths apart. Keeping your legs straight, bend from the waist and reach to the floor.

Don't bounce when stretching. Moving slowly into a stretch works best.

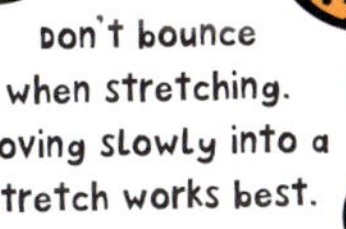

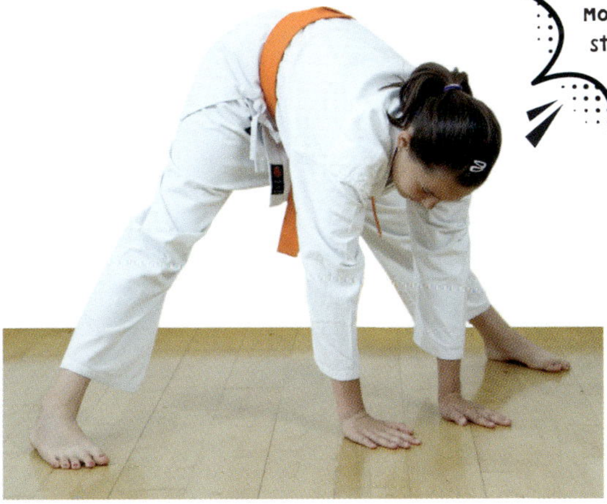

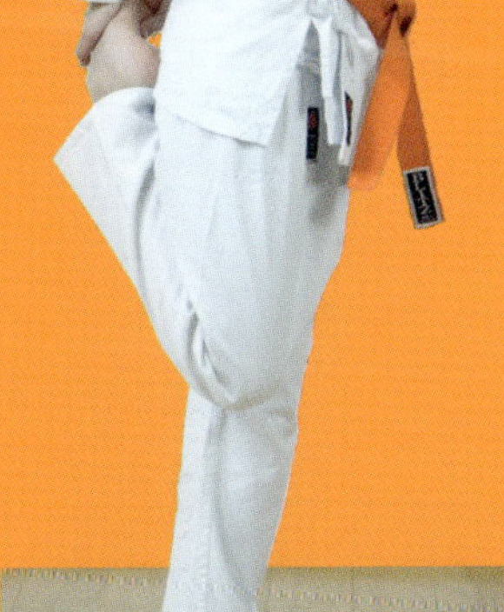

STANCES

Stances are the foundation of karate technique. They are concerned with how you position your legs and body, but the way you position your hands will vary. Making the effort to improve your stances will not only make your karate look better – it will also help to build strong legs, which are the driving force behind strong, fast karate techniques.

FRONT STANCE – ZENKUTSU DACHI

Bend your front knee, putting most of your weight onto your front foot. Ensure that your front foot is pointing forward. Your rear foot should point forward at about 45 degrees.

BACK STANCE – KOKUTSU DACHI

Bend your back leg, putting most of your weight onto your back foot. Ensure that your front foot points forward, and your back foot points out to the side. Your hips should be turned so that they face to the side.

FIGHTING STANCE – KAME

Put most of your weight onto your front foot, as you would in the front stance. Bend both knees and put more weight onto your toes than your heels. Keep your hands up in guard, protecting your body, but ready to punch forward. Your hips should be turned to the side, but your head should face forward.

CAT STANCE – NEKO ASHI DACHI

Bend your back leg and put all of your weight onto your back foot. Bend your front leg slightly.

HORSE-RIDING STANCE – KIBA DACHI

Bend both of your knees so that your weight is evenly distributed between either foot. Both feet should be pointing in the same direction.

PUNCHING

Punching is the most important technique in karate. Karate uses straight punches, which travel directly from your hip to the target.

MAKING A FIST

You need to make a fist correctly so that you do not injure your hands when you punch. NEVER tuck your thumb inside your fingers.

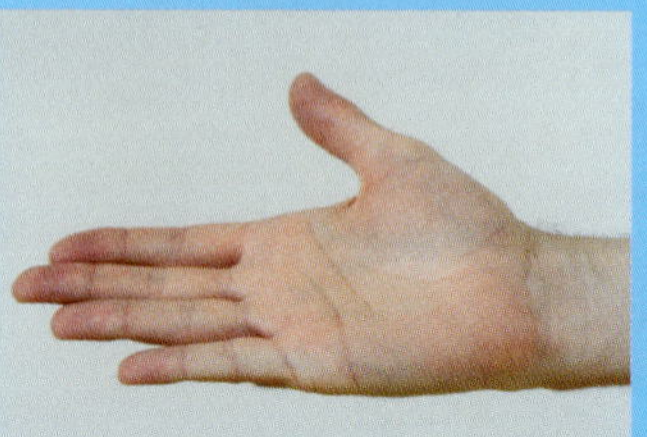

STEP 1

Open your hand.

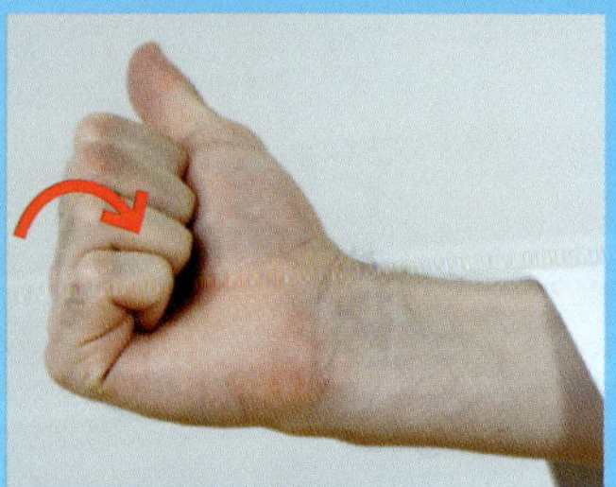

STEP 2

Curl in your fingers tightly.

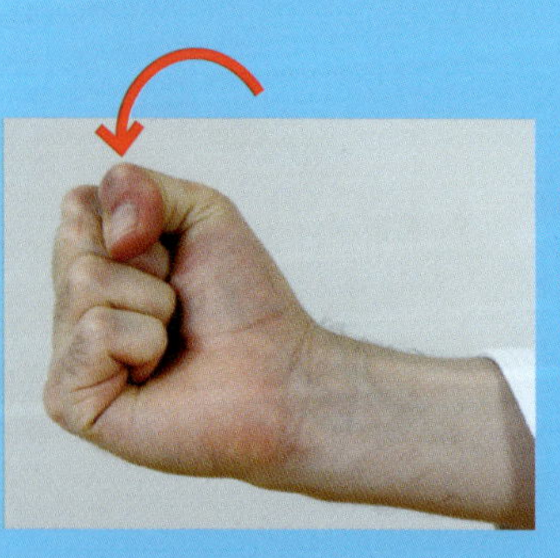

STEP 3

Put your thumb on top of your fingers, tucking it in as much as possible.

STANDING PUNCH – CHOKU-ZUKI

Practice your punching while standing still, so that you can focus on good punching technique.

STEP 1

Start with your hands in fists, held by your hips.

STEP 2

Push your fist forward, keeping your elbow behind the fist.

STEP 3

Straighten your arm and rotate your wrist. Make sure you keep your wrist straight.

STEPPING PUNCH – OI-ZUKI

The stepping punch is used when you need to close the distance between you and your opponent quickly.

STEP 1
Start in front stance.

STEP 2
Slide your rear foot forward so that your feet come together. Start pulling the front hand back, while pushing the punching hand forward.

STEP 3
Keep your foot moving so that you finish in front stance as you complete the punch.

JABBING PUNCH – KIZAMI-ZUKI

The jabbing punch is a fast attack which can be aimed at the head level without compromising your defences. It can be used to test your opponent's defence, or to set up other, more powerful attacks.

Start in fighting posture and punch using the leading hand. Turn your hips so that your chest turns to the side, pushing your leading shoulder forward.

REVERSE PUNCH – GYAKU-ZUKI

The reverse punch is a stronger attack than the jab, but requires more commitment, and can expose you to a counterattack.

Start in the fighting posture and punch using the rear hand. Turn your hips so that your chest faces forwards, pushing your rear shoulder forward.

KICKING

Kicks are the most impressive aspect of karate, but they are also one of the most difficult aspects to master. Kicks require not only great skill and agility, but also strength and flexibility. When sparring, kicks have the disadvantage of being slower than punches and can result in a momentary loss of mobility. However, using your feet to attack leaves your hands free to defend – kicks are your most powerful attack.

FRONT KICK – MAE GERI

The front kick is a very fast kick, and is usually performed with a snapping motion, hitting with the ball of the foot. Sometimes a thrusting motion is used to push the opponent back.

Make sure that you have warmed up your leg muscles before trying any high kicks.

STEP 1

Start in front stance with your arms straight out to the side. Keep your hands in this position throughout the kicking technique.

STEP 2

Lift your knee ready to kick. The higher you lift your knee the higher you can kick.

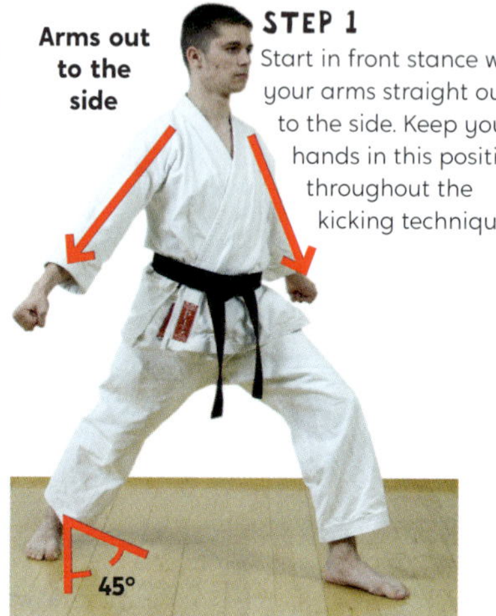

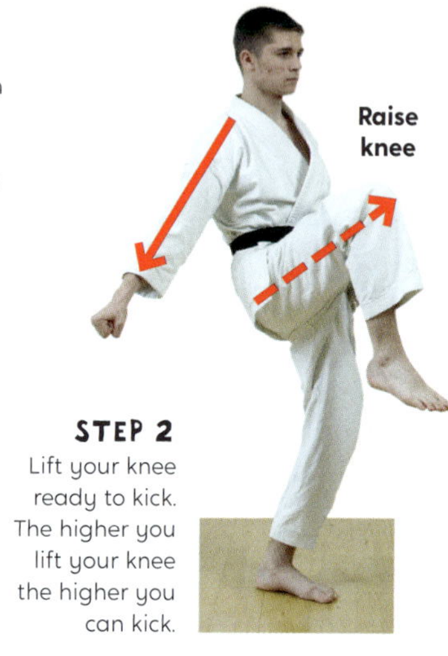

STEP 3

Extend your bent knee, kicking forward. Point the foot forward but pull your toes back, so that you make contact using the ball of your foot.

STEP 4

Immediately snap your foot back. Make sure you don't let the knee drop yet.

STEP 5

Land in front stance.

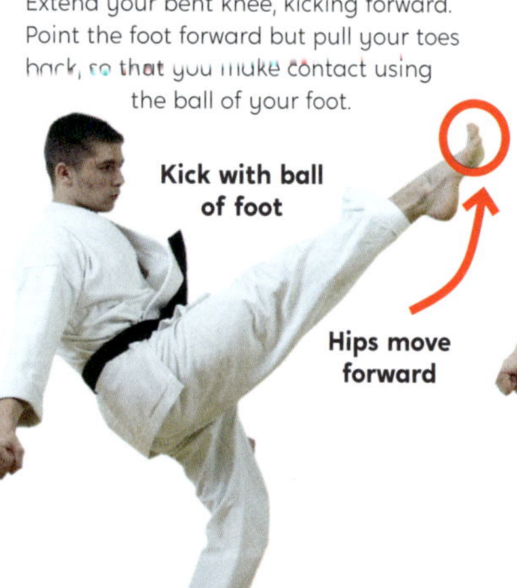

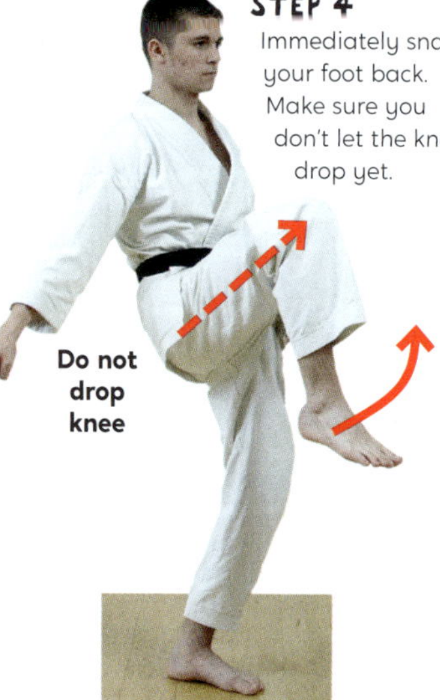

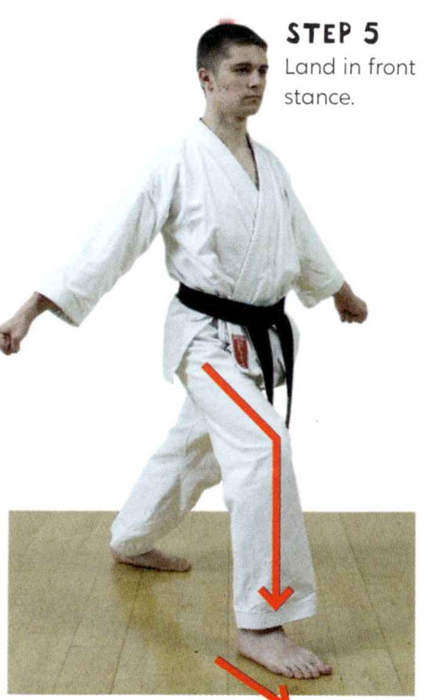

SIDE THRUSTING KICK – YOKO KEKOMI

Because it is a thrusting kick, this side kick can be used as a stopping or pushing kick. In self-defense situations, it can be used as a highly damaging attack to the side or back of an opponent's knee.

STEP 1
Start in horse-riding stance. Put your hands up as a fighting guard, pointing in the direction you are facing.

STEP 2
Step across, one foot in front of the other. Make sure you keep your weight low and your knees bent.

STEP 3
Lift your knee ready to kick. If you lift your leg high, you will be able to kick high.

STEP 4
Thrust your foot out. Turn your hips away from the kick, so that your foot turns sideways and your heel is slightly higher than your toes.

STEP 5
Pull your knee back, as in Step 3.

STEP 6
Step down into horse-riding stance.

SIDE RISING KICK – YOKO KEAGE

This side kick is similar to the side thrusting kick, but is much faster, using a more direct path and a fast push-pull hip action to whip the foot out and then back.

STEP 1
Start in horse-riding stance.

STEP 2
Step across, one foot in front of the other. Make sure you keep your weight low and your knees bent.

STEP 3
Lift the knee of your front leg, so that the foot you are going to kick with rests on your other knee. Point the kicking knee in the direction you are going to kick.

STEP 4
Lift your knee higher and push your hips towards the target while straightening your leg.

STEP 5
Immediately snap the foot back to your knee.

STEP 6
Step down into horse riding stance.

ROUNDHOUSE KICK – MAWASHI GERI

The roundhouse kick (also known as the round or turning kick) is very popular in karate tournaments. Of all the kicks, it is the most likely to score points. Traditionally, it hits with the ball of the foot. However in tournaments, where it is necessary to make safe contact, it is usual to hit with the top surface of the foot.

STEP 1
Start in fighting stance.

STEP 2
Lift your back leg. Angle your kicking leg so that your foot is almost as high as your knee.

STEP 3
Rotate your hips.

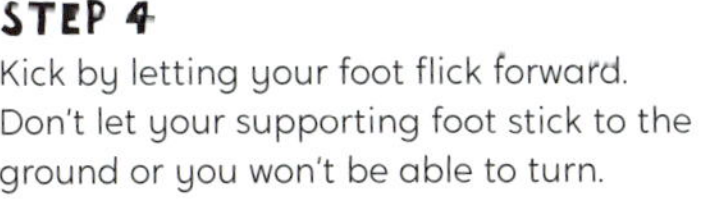

STEP 4
Kick by letting your foot flick forward. Don't let your supporting foot stick to the ground or you won't be able to turn.

STEP 5
Snap the foot back.

STEP 6
Step down into fighting stance.

TOP TIP
Improving flexibility is the key to improving your kicks. If you do **20** minutes of stretching each day you will quickly see improvements in how high you can kick.

BACK KICK – USHIRO GERI
This powerful kick hits with a thrusting action, using the heel.

STEP 1
Start in fighting stance.

STEP 2
Rotate on the spot and lift your back foot. Bring your back leg forward and raise the foot close to the knee of your supporting leg.

STEP 3
Thrust your foot backward in a straight line. Ensure that your kicking leg travels close to your support leg. As you kick, throw your arms in the direction of the kick.

STEP 4
Pull your foot straight back. Make sure that it moves in a straight line, and that your foot finishes on your knee.

HOOK KICK – URA MAWASHI GERI

The hook kick is also known as a reverse roundhouse kick. It is performed as if doing a thrust kick slightly off-target, but then hooking the leg in at the end to hit with your heel. In tournaments where it is necessary to make safe contact, it is usual to hit with the base of the foot.

STEP 1
Start in fighting stance, holding your hands up as a defensive guard.

STEP 2
Lift your front knee, keeping your hands in the guard position.

STEP 3
Twist your hip and kick, hooking your leg in to hit with your heel. To increase the power of the hooking action, you can bend your knee.

STEP 4
Pull your leg back, making sure that you don't let your knee drop. Your leg should come back along the path that you used when kicking.

STEP 5
Step back down into fighting posture.

BLOCKING

In karate, blocking techniques can be used to deflect incoming attacks and are key to defending yourself. These same techniques can be used as effective attacks when directed at an opponent. You can block with either hand, depending on where you expect an attack to come from.

DOWNWARD BLOCK – GEDAN BARAI
This block can be used to deflect low punches or kicks.

STEP 1
Prepare for the block by crossing your arms. Lift your blocking arm so that it is alongside your ear.

STEP 2
Step forward into a front stance and block down. Pull up the opposite fist to your hip. The blocking arm should twist at the end so that your palm faces down.

TOP TIP
Use this checklist to improve your downward block:
- The fist of your blocking hand should finish just above your front knee.
- Your blocking arm should finish straight.
- Make sure your opposite fist is pulled back to your hip.
- Your body should be turned to the side so that you are hiding behind your blocking arm.

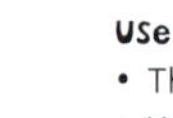

RISING BLOCK – AGE UKE
This block can be used to deflect head-level punches.

STEP 1
Prepare for the block by pulling the blocking hand to your hip and reaching with the opposite hand.

STEP 2
Start blocking as if punching up from the hip, and then vertically in front of your face. At the same time, pull back the opposite hand so that your arms cross.

STEP 3
Step forward into a front stance and complete the block by pushing the elbow up. Pull the opposite fist to your hip.

TOP TIP
Use this checklist to improve your rising block:
- The forearm of your blocking hand should finish just in front of your forehead.
- Your blocking arm should finish bent
- Make sure your opposite fist is pulled back to your hip.
- Your body should be turned to the side so that your blocking arm is pushed forward.

OUTSIDE BLOCK – SOTO UKE

This is a powerful block that can be used to deflect stomach-level punches and thrusting kicks.

STEP 1

Prepare for the block by pulling the blocking hand behind your head, and reaching forward with the opposite hand.

STEP 2

Step forward into a front stance and complete the block by rotating your body and swinging your blocking arm around. Pull the opposite hand to your hip. Rotate the blocking wrist so that your palm faces towards you.

INSIDE BLOCK – UCHI UKE

This block is particularly useful for parrying roundhouse kicks or hooking punches.

STEP 1

Prepare for the block by moving your blocking hand across your body and reaching with the opposite hand.

STEP 2

Step forward into a front stance and complete the block. Pull back the opposite hand to your hip. Twist the blocking wrist so that your palm faces towards you.

TOP TIP

Use this checklist to improve your inside and outside blocks.

- The fist of your blocking hand should finish at the same height as your shoulder.
- Your blocking arm should finish bent 90 degrees.
- Make sure your opposite fist is pulled back to your hip.
- Your body should be turned to the side so that you are hiding behind your blocking arm.

KNIFE HAND BLOCK – SHOTO UKE

This block can be used to deflect stomach-level punches.

STEP 1

Prepare by opening both hands and crossing your arms, lifting your blocking arm so that it is alongside your ear.

STEP 2

Step backwards into a back stance. Bring your blocking hand forward, with your elbow bent and your palm facing outwards. Pull the opposite hand back to the center of your body.

TOP TIP

Use this checklist to improve your knife hand block.

- Hit with the fleshy part of the hand.
- Keep your fingers together.
- Keep your wrist straight.
- Don't let your elbows stick out. Keep them tucked in close to your center line.

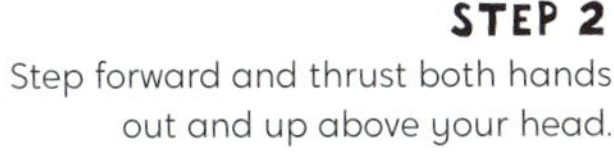

STEP 1

Prepare by opening both hands. Cross your arms at the wrists, in front of your stomach.

CROSS BLOCK – JUJI UKE

This block can be used to parry downward, swinging attacks.

STEP 2

Step forward and thrust both hands out and up above your head.

TOP TIP

Use this checklist to improve your cross block.

- Keep your fingers together.
- Keep your wrists straight.
- Make sure you push the block high enough so any attack goes over your head.

FOOTWORK DRILLS

Good footwork is key to winning karate sparring matches. If you are light on your feet and can move quickly, then you can more easily evade attacks, or hit your opponent when attacking. The key to fast footwork is to keep your weight on the balls of your feet and to keep your legs bent. This is hard that requires strong muscles.

SLIDING JAB

This is a fast attack which can be used to test your opponent's defenses, or as an opening move in a combination. It does not have the range of a stepping punch, but it is faster.

STEP 1
Start in fighting posture, with your weight on your front leg.

STEP 2
Slightly pick up your front foot and push with your back leg. This will propel you forward. Don't transfer weight to your back leg or you won't move as quickly. As you move forward, punch with your front hand.

Front foot slides forward

Arm bends

Back leg slides in

STEP 3
As your weight comes down on your front foot, drag your rear leg and punching arm in, so you finish in fighting stance, ready for your next move.

SLIDING CROSS

This is not as fast as the sliding jab, but if done correctly it can penetrate your opponent's defenses. The key is to use a strong hip motion to drive the punch forward.

Back leg straight

STEP 1
Start in fighting posture with your weight on your front leg.

STEP 2
As with the sliding jab, pick up your front foot slightly and push with your back leg. As you move forward, rotate your hips so your chest faces forwards, and punch with your rear hand to stomach level.

Rear hand punches

Drag rear leg in

Arm bends

STEP 3
As your weight comes down onto your front foot, drag your rear leg and punching arm in. You finish in fighting stance ready for your next move.

SWITCH COUNTER

Use the switch to evade an attack and then immediately counterattack. This takes practice to get right. If you retreat too far, you will not be able to catch your opponent with the counterattack. If you do not retreat far enough, you might fail to evade the attack in the first place.

STEP 1
Start in fighting posture with your weight on your front leg.

STEP 2
Slide your front leg back to meet your other leg while blocking down with your front hand. Try not to transfer too much weight to your back leg.

STEP 3
Step forward with your other leg and punch to either head or stomach level.

THE FAST KICK

If you use the correct footwork you can kick much faster. This footwork can be used with any of the kicks to produce a rapid kick attack. The key is to use your front leg to do the kick, and skip in quickly to close the distance.

STEP 1
Start in fighting posture.

STEP 2
Skip in with your back leg and immediately lift your front knee. Twist your hip to produce a roundhouse kick.

STEP 3
Slide your supporting leg back, and immediately bring your front foot down to take its place.

TOP TIP

When using kicking attacks, make sure you keep your guard up. One of the advantages of using kicks is that your hands are free to defend you.

SPARRING DRILLS

Sparring drills are used to practice attacking and defending with a partner. All karate techniques must be used with appropriate control, which means stopping your attacks just short of actually hitting your partner. This is especially important when performing a head-level attack.

DEFENCE AGAINST HEAD-LEVEL PUNCH

STEP 1

Face your opponent in fighting stance.

STEP 2

As your opponent punches, slide back and deflect the punch above your head with a rising block. Twist your body so that your blocking arm is pushed forward toward the attack. Pull your opposite arm back in preparation for your counterattack.

STEP 3

Punch with your non-blocking hand, rotating your body so that your arm is pushed forwards and can reach your opponent. This is called a reverse punch.

DEFENCE AGAINST MIDDLE-LEVEL PUNCH

STEP 1
Face your opponent in fighting stance.

STEP 2
As your opponent punches, slide back and deflect the punch to the side with an outside block. Twist your body to add extra power to the block. Your opposite arm should be pulled back in preparation for your counterattack. At the end of the blocking motion your body should be turned to the side, so that it is hidden behind your blocking arm.

STEP 3
Rotate your body as you reverse punch, so that your punching arm is pushed forwards far enough to reach your opponent.

TOP TIP
Don't overreach by leaning so that your head comes forward when you punch. If you are too far away, then you need to use your legs to make up the distance.

DEFENCE AGAINST FRONT KICK

STEP 1

Face your opponent in fighting stance.

Put most of your weight onto your front foot, as you would in the front stance. Bend both knees and put more weight onto your toes than your heels. Keep your hands up in guard, protecting your body, but ready to punch forward. Your hips should be turned to the side, but your head should face forward.

STEP 2

As your opponent kicks, evade by sliding to the side and hitting the inside of the leg with a downward block. Don't try to parry the kick – you will not be able to safely stop such a strong attack with direct force. Instead, use your body motion as your main defense and aim for your block to make contact with the side or underside of the kicking leg.

STEP 3

Reverse punch to the stomach. Remember to turn your hips in order to reach your opponent. If this is not enough, then you can slide forward to reach further.

DEFENCE AGAINST SIDE KICK

STEP 1

Face your opponent in fighting stance.

STEP 2

As your opponent kicks, evade by sliding to the side and hitting the back of the leg with an outside block. However, you should not try to reach the kick if it was very low or off target, as you will lose your posture.

STEP 3

Counterattack with a reverse punch to the stomach. If you made contact with your block then you may have pushed your opponent off-balance. In this case you will be able to counterattack with a reverse punch aimed at their back.

TOP TIP

When blocking a kick, you must use body motion to evade the kick. If you try to block head-on using brute force alone, you will risk bruising your arm.

DEFENCE AGAINST ROUNDHOUSE KICK

STEP 1

Face your opponent in fighting stance.

Put most of your weight onto your front foot, as you would in the front stance. Bend both knees and put more weight onto your toes than your heels. Keep your hands up in guard, protecting your body, but ready to punch forward. Your hips should be turned to the side, but your head should face forward.

STEP 2

As your opponent kicks, evade by sliding away from the kick and ward off the leg with an inside block. Rotate your body and swing your blocking arm around. Make sure that you keep your blocking arm tense at the point of impact in order to stop this kick.

STEP 3

As your opponent steps forward after the kick, counterattack with a reverse punch aimed at the stomach.

DEFENCE AGAINST BACK KICK

STEP 1

Face your opponent in fighting stance.

Put most of your weight onto your front foot, as you would in the front stance. Bend both knees and put more weight onto your toes than your heels. Keep your hands up in guard, protecting your body, but ready to punch forward. Your hips should be turned to the side, but your head should face forward.

STEP 2

This kick is very hard to stop, but quite easy to deflect. So, as your opponent kicks, evade by sliding to the side and deflecting the leg with an outside block. With practice, you will find that you will even be able to move in close to your opponent when performing this defense, as long as you move off the line of the attack.

STEP 3

Your opponent will step forwad after the kick, and will find that they have moved past you. You are now to their side, in what is called a flanking position. Counterattack with a reverse punch to the back, or the ribs.

DIET

Eating healthily for both karate training and karate competitions can give you the edge. It can improve your performance by making sure that you have plenty of energy for physical activity.

BEFORE TRAINING

Before training, you should eat carbohydrates, which are good energy foods.

Karate training sessions normally last between one and two hours. Snacks eaten within an hour before exercise should keep you from feeling hungry. Karate competitions, on the other hand, tend to be all-day events with many breaks. So it's best to keep snacks that are high in carbohydrates, such as bananas and sandwiches, close at hand.

DURING TRAINING

Karate can be hot work, so it's important to stay hydrated.

It is a good idea to hydrate before beginning any exercise, and then to re-hydrate regularly after the first 30 minutes of exercise. Water is suitable for short training sessions. Sports drinks that contain sugars are more effective for longer training sessions.

MENTAL ATTITUDE

Physical training is only part of karate. An essential component is your mental attitude. Training to become a black belt, and training for competitions requires patience and dedication. Karate performances can be determined by how confident you look.

AWARENESS

You should be aware of your surroundings and your opponent. The Japanese call this *zanshin*. You need to be aware of an imminent attack in order react to it and to defend yourself.

OPEN MIND

Being aware of an imminent attack is not enough. You must also be in the correct state of mind in order to react to that attack. This means that you need to have an open mind, which is able to react to any attack. The Japanese call this *mushin*. If you build a plan around only one particular attack, then you will be unable to act quickly if that expectation is wrong. Fear is a barrier to an open, reactive mind. Through karate training you will be able to overcome the fear of being hit, and this will enable you to react quickly.

DON'T PANIC!

Stay calm and focused. Never lose your temper. Karate requires that you use focused aggression, not anger. People who get angry act foolishly and without forward thinking, and are easily defeated.

PERSEVERANCE

Training to become a black belt can take anywhere between three and five years. A typical student will train two to three times a week for this duration of time. Therefore, to become a proficient martial artist takes many years of training and commitment. Staying motivated and on track to achieve this goal is essential. Karate training is mostly about repeating moves until they start to become natural reactions.

STRONG SPIRIT

A strong spirit and positive mental attitude will enable you to overcome setbacks and challenges. One method used by karate practitioners to build spirit is to use a martial shout called a *kiai*. Using a strong kiai when you attack will build your courage and spirit, while working to intimidate your opponent.

COURTESY AND RESPECT

You should be polite to everyone and that includes your opponents. If you do not have respect for your opponent's abilities, then you are in danger of underestimating them.

GLOSSARY

Counter – An attack used in response to or to block an opponent's attack.

Evade – To dodge an attack.

Fighting stance – An informal fighting stance with the arms ready to attack or defend and the legs bent to allow for rapid movement.

Front stance – A formal posture often used for lunge attacks with most of the weight on the front knee.

Hamstring – A tendon in the back of the knee.

Jab – A fast punch using the leading hand.

Kata – Traditional forms usually consisting of between 20 and 110 choreographed moves, as if fighting a series of imaginary opponents.

Parry – Defending against an attacking move.

Quad – This is short for quadricep, a muscle on the front of the thigh.

Spar – To fight in a stylized way, without putting your full strength into attacks.

Sweep – A leg technique intended to knock an opponent's foot or lower leg in order to unbalance them.

Throw – A grappling move whereby an opponent is unbalanced and is forced to fall to the ground.

INDEX

B
blocking 16-21

D
diet 30
drills 22-29

F
fist 8
footwork 22-23

K
kata 3
kiai 31

kicking 10-15
kihon 3
kumite 3

M
mental attitude 30-31

O
Okinawa 3
origins of karate 3

P
punching 8-9

S
self-defense 3, 11
sparring 24-29
stances 6-7
stretching 4-5, 13

T
tournaments 13, 15

W
warming up 4-5

Y
yame 9